D0239599

Y̶ Eat
ss!

For my mum and dad ~
GR
For my sister,
who meets every adventure with panache ~
SM

First published in 2010 by Scholastic Children's Books
Euston House, 24 Eversholt Street
London NW1 1DB
a division of Scholastic Ltd
www.scholastic.co.uk
London ~ New York ~ Toronto ~ Sydney ~ Auckland
Mexico City ~ New Delhi ~ Hong Kong

Text copyright © 2010 Gillian Rogerson
Illustrations copyright © 2010 Sarah McIntyre

HB ISBN 978 1407 10560 4
PB ISBN 978 1407 10561 1

You Can't Eat a Princess!

Written by
Gillian Rogerson

Illustrated by
Sarah McIntyre

SCHOLASTIC

"It's nearly time for my party!"
said Princess Spaghetti.

"Is everything ready?

"Chocolate spread sandwiches – **yes.**

Extra thick chocolate milkshakes – **yes.**

An enormous chocolate birthday cake – **yes.**

One **King**, waiting to greet the guests…

"No!" King Cupcake's throne was empty,
except for a note.

We have taken your king.
You will never find us.
We come from another planet.
HA HA!

"Oh no!"
cried Princess Spaghetti. "King Cupcake has been kidnapped by aliens!"

Princess Spaghetti summoned the Royal Knights.

"One of you will have to rescue King Cupcake," she said.

"Don't look at **me**," sniffed the first Royal Knight. "I can't possibly go out in this weather. **I'll catch a cold.**"

"I'm in the middle of knitting a jumper for my teddy," whinged the second Royal Knight. "I can't stop now."

"Well, I can't go," fussed the third Royal Knight. "Have you seen my hair? I've still got my curlers in!"

"Very well then," said Princess Spaghetti. "I guess I'll have to go myself."

And she scooted off to the Royal Garage where she found the Royal Rocket.

She climbed aboard.

"Goodness! Look at all these buttons!
Which one should I press?" she wondered.
"I'll just press them **all**."
The Royal Rocket moved to the left,
then the right and finally…

...up and away into space!

Princess Spaghetti steered the Royal Rocket

between sparkling stars and strangely shaped planets.

"Father must be here somewhere," she told herself.

Just then a shooting star whizzed past –

Whizz!

ZOOM!

followed by a speeding comet –

Princess Spaghetti tried to avoid them and swerved to the side,

but the rocket began to spin uncontrollably.

Princess Spaghetti grabbed the controls and squealed,

"I'll have to make an emergency landing!"

She landed neatly on the nearest planet.
A group of aliens were looking up at her and smiling.

"Hello,
I'm Princess Spaghetti,"
she said, with a polite curtsey.

"Welcome to our planet,"
said one alien. "We love
princesses here."

"I like mine with chips," said
another alien.

"I like mine on toast with
a bit of ketchup," said a third.

"Yum,
yum."

"You can't eat a princess!" said Princess Spaghetti.
"I'm looking for my father, King Cupcake.
Have you seen him?"

The aliens shook their heads.
But Princess Spaghetti wasn't convinced.

She looked closer at the aliens, and gasped.
"You're wearing King Cupcake's crown!
Have you eaten my dad?"

"Not yet," grinned the alien, licking his lips.

"Take me to him **at once!**" demanded Princess Spaghetti.
The aliens were getting worried. They didn't like their
dinner shouting at them, so they led her to a large
cooking pot. King Cupcake was inside.

"**Father!**" cried Princess Spaghetti.
"What are you **doing** in there?"

"I'm having a swim. The water's lovely and warm," said King Cupcake.

"But Father," she said, "these aliens are planning to **eat** you!

Well, I won't let them!"

She pointed to the nearest alien and said,
"Get my father out at **once!**"
The aliens didn't move.

Princess Spaghetti had had **enough!**

OW!"

she commanded in her most princessy voice.

The aliens knew they
had met their match.

King Cupcake was helped out of the pot.

Princess Spaghetti gave him a big hug.

"What are we going to eat now?" asked a worried alien.

"How about some chocolate?" suggested Princess Spaghetti.

"What's chocolate?" asked the alien.

Princess Spaghetti was shocked.

"You've never had **chocolate**?

You must come with me at once!"

The aliens were too frightened to disobey

her, so they followed Princess Spaghetti home.

Princess Spaghetti finally arrived at her party.

"Try this," she said kindly, giving each alien
a huge piece of chocolate cake.

"Delicious!" said the first alien who tried it.
Then he fainted with joy.

"Now that you know how wonderful chocolate is, you'll
never have to eat a person again!" said Princess Spaghetti.

"I would," one of the aliens whispered to his friend, "if they were covered in chocolate!"